SERIOUSLY SILLY

SCARY
FAIRY TALES

GHOSTYSHOCKS
and the THREE MUMMIES

Laurence Anholt
& Arthur Robins

ORCHARD

www.anholt.co.uk

GOOD EVENING, LADIES AND GENTLEMEN.

My name is
THE MAN WITHOUT A HEAD.

Of course I have a head really... it's just that my head is removable. It makes it so much easier to brush my teeth.

So, you like SCARY STORIES, do you? Well, I warn you, the stories I am about to tell are so TERRIFYING that grown men have been known to do wee-wees in their panties.

This story is about a girl named Ghostyshocks, who made the mistake of MESSING WITH A MUMMY and got herself all wound up.

Are you sitting comfortably, tremble-buddies? Then I'll begin.

Tonight's tale is...

GHOSTYSHOCKS and the THREE MUMMIES...

There was once a girl named Ghostyshocks.

She lived with her mother and father and her baby brother in a big tent in the shade of some palm trees in the desert. The family were very poor, but they had a lovely life.

Ghostyshocks could swim in the oasis, or make sandcastles, or relax in her deckchair eating dates, which were her favourite.

In fact, there was only one thing the children were NOT allowed to do.

"You must never, never, never ride a camel into the endless desert," said their father.

"That's right," said their mother. "You will certainly get lost and you might even die of thirst."

"Even worse than that," said their father, "you may end up near the pyramids and you know who lives there..."

"Who lives in the pyramids?" whispered Ghostyshocks.

"Don't even ask!" said her mother and father together.

So, Ghostyshocks stayed near the tent, eating dates and playing with her pet camel (he never took the hump).

One day, it was her mother's birthday. Ghostyshocks was too poor to buy a present, but she was a kind girl.

"You two go out for the day," she told her mother and father. "I'll stay here and look after my brother. Don't worry, I am quite grown up now."

"You won't ride your camel into the… you know…" said her mother.

"No. I won't go into the desert," said Ghostyshocks.

"And you won't go near the… you know…" said her father.

"No. I won't go near the pyramids," said Ghostyshocks.

So they all said goodbye and Ghostyshocks took out a storybook to read to her baby brother.

But her brother was being very naughty. He kept running in and out of the tent with his nappy dangling all around his fat little legs.

"Ghostyshocks, Ghostyshocks, my nappy has come undone," he squealed.

Ghostyshocks put a new nappy on her baby
brother, then she had a little rest in the shade.

When she woke up, her brother had gone!

Ghostyshocks searched high and low, but she couldn't find him anywhere. "Oh dear!" squealed Ghostyshocks. "Whatever will I do?"

What else could she do, Fans of Fear? The one thing she had promised not to do. Ghostyshocks put a bottle of lemonade and some suncream in a bag, threw a saddle on her pet camel (he never took the hump) and set off into the endless desert.

"My poor baby brother," she said. "He will surely die in the hot sun."

All day she rode and, as the sun went down, Ghostyshocks came to a strange stone building in the shape of a triangle.

"Oh dear," she wailed, "I hope this is not the terrible pyramid my father warned me about. Now who was it who lives here?"

Ghostyshocks tied up her pet camel (he never took the hump) and walked all around, but she couldn't find a door.

At last, she climbed right to the top of the pyramid. There was a strange stone carving with a picture of a man playing a trumpet.

It said 'This is the tomb of the king – Toot and Come In'.

Suddenly the tip of the pyramid flipped open. Ghostyshocks peered inside. She called for her baby brother, but there was no answer. She leaned over a bit further…

Suddenly, Ghostyshocks tumbled head over heels inside the cold, dark pyramid.

She landed with a bump in a triangular kitchen. On a stone table were three bowls. In the bowls were some juicy dates, and Ghostyshocks felt very, very hungry.

"I'll just try a few dates," she said. "I'm sure nobody will mind."

First, she tried the big bowl, but the dates were so big they didn't fit in her mouth.

Then she tried the middle-sized bowl, but the dates were too sweet and sticky.

Last of all, she tried the teeny-weeny baby bowl, and the dates were exactly right, so she ate every one and spat the stones in the bowl.

Ghostyshocks looked around. She saw some stone steps going deep down inside the pyramid. She felt very nervous, but she had to find her baby brother. It looked dark down there, but Ghostyshocks found a burning torch.

She tiptoed down the cold stone steps until she reached a spooky triangular room with weird paintings on the walls. But she couldn't find her baby brother.

Ghostyshocks was just about to run back up the stairs, when she noticed something amazing in a corner. She couldn't believe her eyes! There was a huge pile of shiny jewels, glittering bracelets, and golden necklaces.

"Oh!" said Ghostyshocks. "Treasure! I'll just put on one of those necklaces. Nobody will mind."

First, she tried on a big necklace, but that was so long it dragged on the floor.

Then she tried a middle-sized necklace, but that was so heavy she almost fell over.

Then she tried a teeny-weeny golden necklace and some teeny-weeny sparkling bracelets and they fitted perfectly.

Suddenly Ghostyshocks felt tired. She saw three nicely painted sarcophaguses with their lids open.

"I'll just have a little nap," she said, yawning. "Nobody will mind."

She put down the torch and climbed in the huge sarcophagus, but that was far too big.

Next, she climbed in the middle-sized sarcophagus, but that was far too soft.

Then she climbed in the teeny-weeny sarcophagus and that was exactly right. So she shut the lid and fell fast asleep, and dreamed about the endless desert.

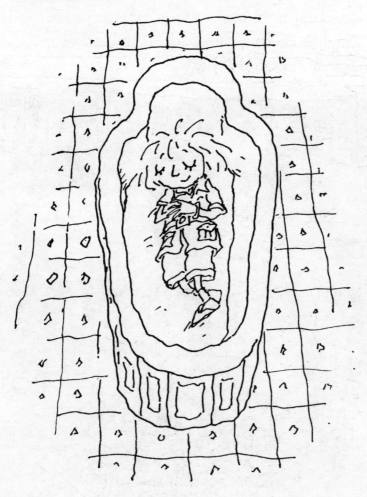

While she was sleeping, the mummies who lived in the pyramid had been out for a thousand-year walk. Now they were hungry. They wanted their breakfast.

They walked slowly, slowly, slowly across the desert under the stars – a huge, tall daddy mummy, a middle-sized mummy mummy and, on her shoulders, a teeny-weeny baby mummy.

The three mummies climbed slowly, slowly, slowly into the pyramid. They looked at all the date stones on the kitchen floor.

"SOMEONE'S BEEN EATING MY DATES!" roared the huge, tall daddy mummy.

"SOMEONE'S BEEN EATING MY DATES!" groaned the middle-sized mummy mummy.

But the teeny-weeny baby mummy was wrapped up so tight, that all he could do was point and say,

Then the three mummies walked slowly, slowly, slowly down the cold stone steps.

"SOMEONE'S BEEN PLAYING WITH MY JEWELS!" roared the huge, tall daddy mummy.

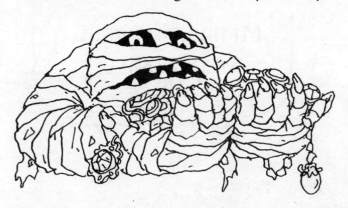

"SOMEONE'S BEEN PLAYING WITH MY JEWELS!" groaned the middle-sized mummy mummy.

But the teeny weeny baby mummy was wrapped up so tight, that all he could do was point and say,

Then the three mummies walked slowly, slowly, slowly towards the sarcophaguses.

"SOMEONE'S BEEN SLEEPING IN MY SARCOPHAGUS!" roared the huge, tall daddy mummy.

"SOMEONE'S BEEN SLEEPING IN MY SARCOPHAGUS!" groaned the middle-sized mummy mummy.

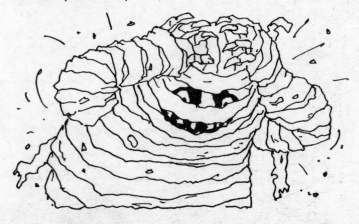

But the teeny-weeny baby mummy was wrapped up so tight, that all he could do was point at the little sarcophagus and say,

Just then, Ghostyshocks woke up. She pushed
open the lid and saw the three mummies –

"EEEEEEeeEEEEEE
EEEEEEEEEEEEEEEE
EEEEEK!!!!"

she screamed. "I WANT MY MUMMY!"

The three mummies walked towards her, slowly, slowly, slowly. Ghostyshocks hopped out of the sarcophagus and ran up the cold stone steps into the kitchen. She looked up at the door, but it was far too high for her to reach.

She could hear the mummies coming slowly, slowly, slowly behind her. So she hopped onto the table.

Suddenly, the teeny weeny baby mummy came running into the kitchen. His bandages were dangling all around his fat little legs.

"EEEEEEEEEEEEEEeeeEEEEEEEEEK!!!!"

screamed Ghostyshocks. "I want my mummy!"

"Ghostyshocks, Ghostyshocks, my nappy has come undone," said the teeny-weeny baby.

Have you guessed, Fans of Fear? It was not a teeny-weeny baby mummy. How could you think such a foolish thing? No this was Ghostyshocks' naughty little baby brother.

You see, the huge, tall daddy mummy and
the middle sized mummy mummy had been
walking in the endless desert when they found
Ghostyshocks' baby brother out on his own, with
his nappy dangling all around his fat little legs.

They loved babies and had wanted one for
thousands of years. Of course, they didn't want
him to get burnt by the hot sun, so they wrapped
him up nice and tight in bandages and carried
him slowly, slowly, slowly back to their nice
cold pyramid.

And now the two mummies were coming slowly, slowly, slowly up the stairs and they were very, very angry. They were angry because someone had taken their dates and they were even angrier because someone had helped herself to their lovely glittering bracelets and jewels and most of all, Fans of Fear, the mummies were furious because someone had been sleeping in their sarcophagus.

The daddy mummy and the mummy mummy came slowly, slowly, slowly into the triangular kitchen. They reached our their horrible bandaged hands, when, quick as a flash, Ghostyshocks picked up her little brother, lifted him up and pushed him through the lid of the pyramid.

The big, tall daddy mummy stretched out to grab her, but just then, Ghostyshocks saw the long bandage dangling from above. She climbed up as quickly as she could and slammed the lid of the pyramid.

Then Ghostyshocks and her baby brother,
hopped onto her pet camel (he never took the
hump) and galloped back across the desert as fast
as they could go.

When their mother and father came back from their birthday outing, they found Ghostyshocks and her baby brother, lying peacefully in a deckchair finishing their storybook.

You see, Fans of Fear, after a long night with the mummies, it was time to relax and unwind. You could say the children were wrapped up in a story.

SERIOUSLY SILLY

SCARY
FAIRY TALES

LAURENCE ANHOLT & ARTHUR ROBINS

Cinderella at the Vampire Ball   PB 978 1 40832 954 2

Jack and the Giant Spiderweb   PB 978 1 40832 957 3

Hansel and Gretel and the Space Witch   PB 978 1 40832 960 3

Snow Fright and the Seven Skeletons   PB 978 1 40832 963 4

Ghostyshocks and the Three Mummies   PB 978 1 40832 966 5

Tom Thumb, the Tiny Spook   PB 978 1 40832 969 6

COLLECT THEM ALL!

Also available as an ebook